KT-484-825

for Eva
D.C.

for Clémence
S.B.

MYRIAD BOOKS LIMITED
35 Bishopsthorpe Road, London SE26 4PA

First published in 2000 by
MIJADE PUBLICATIONS
16-18, rue de l'Ouvrage
5000 Namur-Belgium

© Dona Casarin, 2000
© Stéphanie Blanchart, 2000

Translation: Lisa Pritchard

Dona Casarin and Stephanie Blanchart have asserted their rights to be identified
as the author and illustrator of this work in accordance with the Copyright, Designs
and Patents Act, 1988.

All rights reserved. No part of this publication may be reproduced, stored in a retrieval
system, or transmitted, in any form or by any means electronic, mechanical, photocopying
or otherwise, without prior permission of the copyright owner.

ISBN 1 847460 34 8

Printed in China

The Lost Teddy

By Dona Casarin and Stéphanie Blanchart

MYRIAD BOOKS LIMITED

It is so difficult to choose. Paddington? Pooh? Pingu?

Martin is just right for Eva.

Martin is Eva's first toy.

When Eva learns to walk, Martin does too.

When Eva eats her
supper, Martin does too.
He likes pasta and milk.

When Martin gets dirty,
Eva gives him a good wash.
That's better!

Eva takes Martin everywhere. She gives him presents, looks after him when he is ill. Eva loves Martin very much!

When Eva is sad or tired, all she wants
is a cuddle with Martin and Mummy.

Eva's a big girl now. She's off to
school. Martin comes too of course!
Eva holds his hand.

Martin follows Eva everywhere –
in class and in the playground.

But one day at school,
Eva lets go of Martin's paw. Oh no!

When Eva turns round Martin has gone.
She cries and cries when Daddy comes to pick her up.

All the other children hunt for Martin.

They look everywhere.

They all draw posters and stick them up. Everywhere.

But Martin is nowhere to be found. He has disappeared!

At home, Eva doesn't want to play.
She doesn't want a cuddle. She just
wants Martin.

Mum and Dad try to cheer Eva up but they can't bring
Martin back. He's gone, completely disappeared.

Eva says, "Maybe we'll find him tomorrow." Mum says, "I don't know."

"Maybe another little boy or girl is playing with him," says Mum.

"But he's mine!" says Eva sadly.

Eva waits and waits but Martin
doesn't come back.

Eva likes looking at Martin's picture.
"Oh Mum," she sighs. "I do miss Martin."

Eva doesn't give up.
"Maybe tomorrow
we'll find him!"

Eva waits and waits. Then one day she says to her Mum:

"I think I know what happened to Martin."

"I think Martin went to see Father Christmas, and he decided to give Martin to another little girl who didn't have any other toys."

So Eva picks up Fred Bear.

He's not Martin, but he is very cuddly.

"From now on, Fred, you're going to be my special friend."